Finn MacCool and the Giant's Causeway

Malachy Doyle and Peter Utton

W

Chapter 1:
Finn Shows Off!

"I am the strongest giant in the whole wide world!" roared Finn MacCool, the mighty Irishman.
He was so loud that his voice travelled all the way across the water to Scotland.

"Oh no you're not!" boomed Benandonner, from the other side of the sea. "I'm loads stronger than you!"

To show Finn how strong he was, Benandonner picked up a gigantic boulder from the Scottish shore and lobbed it over towards Ireland. The rock flew over the waves and came crashing down into the sea, right in front of Finn MacCool. SPLASH! It soaked him to the skin.

Chapter 2:
The Causeway

"Anything you can do, I can do better!" roared a furious Finn. He pulled an enormous rock out of the ground and hurled it, with all his might, back towards Scotland.

Benandonner tossed another one and Finn did the same. So that soon, where the rocks landed, there were the beginnings of a path, or causeway, across the Irish Sea.

Una, Finn's wife (who was only the size of a normal human), heard all the fuss and came running down to the shore.

"Finn! Finn!" she cried, tugging on her husband's leg. "Benandonner's twice your size! Stop picking a fight with him, or he'll be over here like a shot and have you for his breakfast!"

"Twice my size, you say?" said the Irish giant, looking out at the ever-growing causeway between the two lands. "At this rate he'll be here by morning, then!"

Now Una might have been a whole heap smaller than Finn, but she was a whole heap cleverer, too.

"Just stop chucking rocks at him!" she said. "I'll go away and see if I can come up with a plan."

Chapter 3: Baby Finn

When Finn wandered back up to the house, there was Una, holding a gigantic nightie and an enormous frilly cap.

"Look what I've made, Finn," she said. "Here, put these on."

"No way!' said Finn. "Everyone will think I'm a baby!"

"That's exactly what I want," said Una.

So Finn did as he was told, and then Una led him into the back room and showed him a massive cradle.

"Get in here," she told him, "and wait!"

Finn lay down in the cradle, and soon he was deeply dozing.

Meanwhile Una baked two massive cakes, and in one of them she hid a rod of iron.

Next morning, at daybreak, the mighty Benandonner picked his way across the new path, all the way from Scotland.
Boom, boom, boom! went the sound of his feet on the rocks.
Una gasped at the sight of him, for he was bigger – much bigger – than Finn.

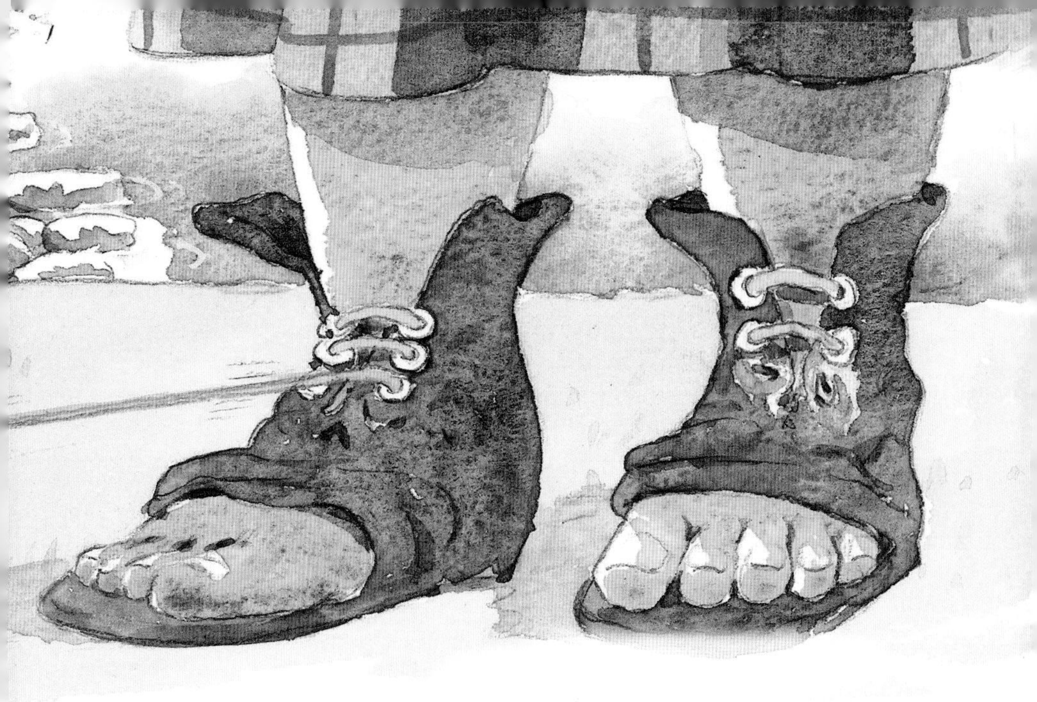

"Where's Finn MacCool?" boomed the Scottish giant, pounding on Una's door.
"He's gone over to sort out that big bully, Benandonner," cried Una, through the letterbox.
"But I'm Benandonner!" roared the furious giant. "And I'm here to sort HIM out!"
"Oh dear," said Una, popping outside. "Well, you'll have to wait till he's back, then. I'm sure he won't be long."

Chapter 4:
Una's Plan

"While you're here you can
do me a favour, big man,"
said Una. "The wind's rattling
the door. Could you turn the house round,
like Finn always does when it's noisy
like this?"
"Anything Finn can do, I can do better,"
said Benandonner, wrapping his two
massive arms around the house.
But it was built deep into the rock.

Una watched as he huffed and he puffed. She did a little smile as he puffed and he huffed. At last the great ugly giant managed to pull the house up and out of the ground, turn it around, and put it back down again.

"You say Finn does that every time the wind blows?" said the mighty fellow, exhausted. "Oh yes," said Una, handing him a handkerchief to mop his brow. "Isn't he the kind husband?"

She brought Benandonner out one of the cakes she'd baked.

"Here, have one of these," she said. "You look like you might be hungry, after all that hard work."

She gave Benandonner the cake with the iron bar in.

The Scottish giant bit down on it and …
“AARRGGH!” he yelled, spitting out broken teeth. “What in the name of goodness did you put in there?”
“Oh, Finn likes them crunchy,” said Una, hiding another smile. “But stop your yelling, man – you’ll wake the baby!”

ARRGH!

Just then there was a mighty roar,
"WAAA!" from the cradle.
"Good grief!" said Benandonner, running to see what sort of a child could make such an enormous sound. He was even more shocked when he saw the size of the massive infant.

"How big is your husband, Finn,"
he said, trembling,
"if that's his baby?"

"Big," said Una, not even bothering to hide her grin this time. "Bigger than you!" She reached into the cradle and gave the baby the second cake – the one without the iron bar in.

The baby munched. The baby crunched.

The baby munched and crunched
and burped.

"More!" he yelled. "More! MORE!"

"He has a fine set of teeth on him, to be sure," said Una, proudly. "Put your finger in and feel them, Benandonner!"

The giant drew back.

"Or are you scared?" said Una.
"Who, me?" said the Scottish giant. "I'm not scared of ANYONE!"

Chapter 5:
Benandonner's Strength

He put his middle finger in the baby's mouth and …
CRUNCH! Finn bit it, clean off!

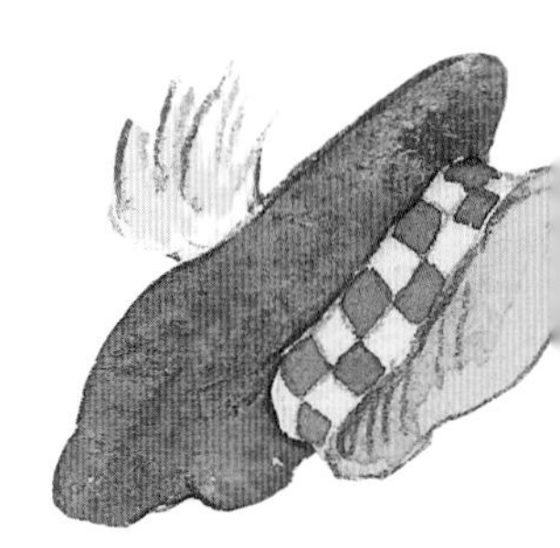

"AARRGGH!" cried Benandonner. "He's bitten off my middle finger, and that's where I keep my strength!"

As he lost his power, he lost his size. So, like a balloon going down, he got smaller and smaller until soon he was only the size of a rabbit.

"I'm out of here before Finn gets back," he peeped. "I've no chance against him now!"

Then he was off, over The Giant's Causeway, and he never set foot in Ireland again.

If you go to The Giant's Causeway, in Northern Ireland, or to Staffa, on the west coast of Scotland, you'll see what's left of the path the giants made, sticking up out of the sea. It's there to this day.

About the story

Finn MacCool is a legendary Irish figure – the last leader of the Fianna – a warrior group. He doesn't always appear as a giant. His many adventures are told in a long story believed to be from the 12th century CE. Finn was the son of a king, but was brought up secretly in the forest by a warrior woman. He got the gift of knowledge while studying with the poet Finnegas. Finnegas had been fishing for the salmon of knowledge in the River Boyne for years. Finally, he catches it and asks Finn to cook it. Finn burns his thumb on the fish, and sucks it. In doing so, he gains all the knowledge in the world! According to legend, Finn never died and still sleeps in a cave beneath Ireland.

Be in the story!

Imagine you are Finn MacCool when Una tells you to dress as a baby and get into the cot. What might you be thinking?

Now imagine you are Benandonner. Una has invited you back to see Baby Finn. Write a letter to her saying if you would like to come or not, and why.

First published in 2014 by
Franklin Watts
338 Euston Road
London
NW1 3BH

Franklin Watts Australia
Level 17/207 Kent Street
Sydney
NSW 2000

A CIP catalogue record for this book is available
from the British Library.

The artwork for this story first appeared in
Hopscotch Adventures: Finn MacCool and the Giant's Causeway

ISBN 978 1 4451 3369 0 (hbk)
ISBN 978 1 4451 3370 6 (pbk)
ISBN 978 1 4451 3372 0 (library ebook)
ISBN 978 1 4451 3371 3 (ebook)

Series Editor: Jackie Hamley
Series Advisor: Catherine Glavina
Series Designer: Cathryn Gilbert

Printed in China

Franklin Watts is a divison of
Hachette Children's Books,
an Hachette UK company.
www.hachette.co.uk